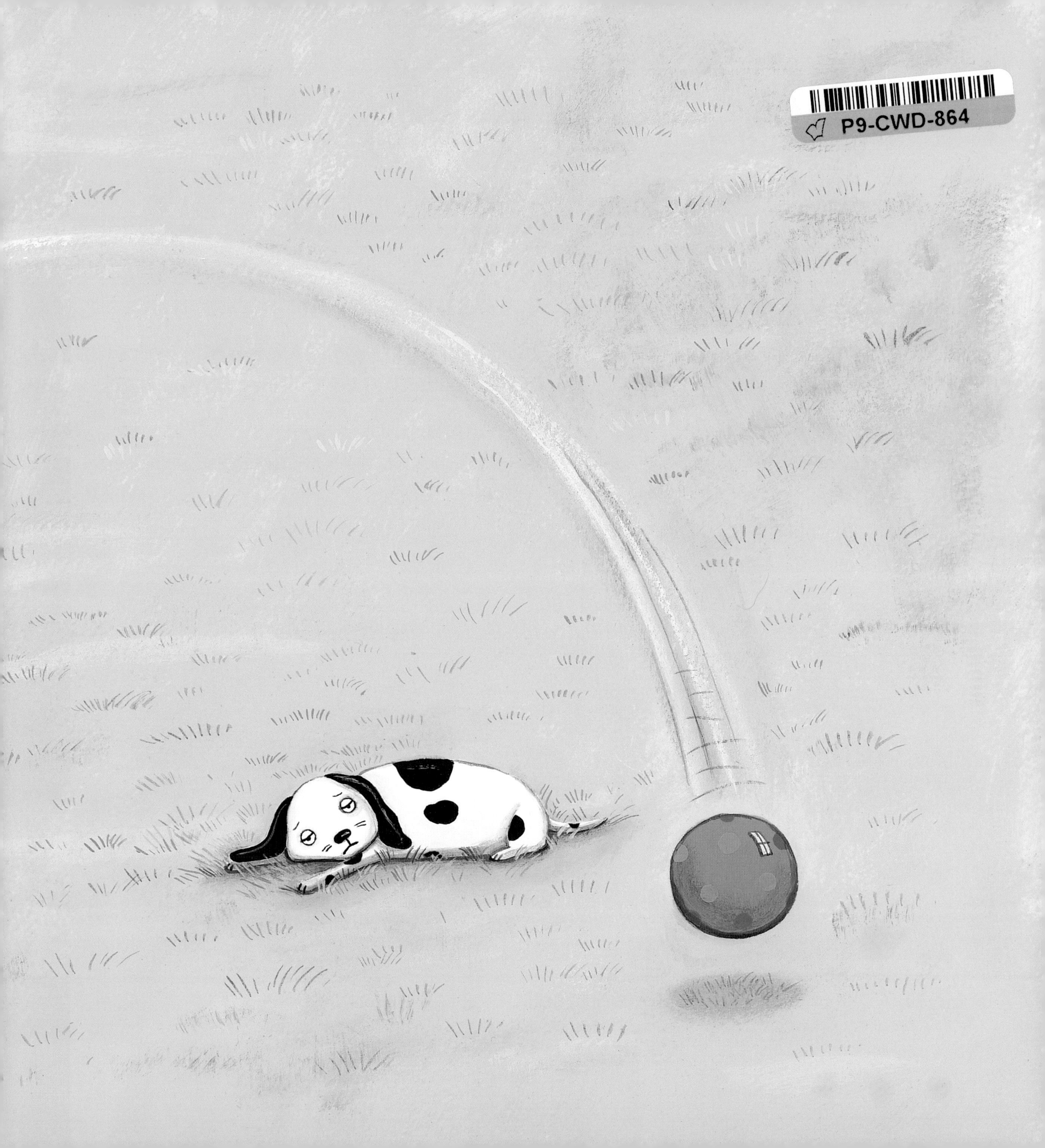

Dedicated to Bill Flannery...
who was never bored or boring
—LP

tiger tales
an imprint of ME Media, LLC
202 Old Ridgefield Road, Wilton, CT 06897
Published in the United States 2006
Originally published in Great Britain 2005
By Little Tiger Press
An imprint of Magi Publications
Text and illustrations copyright © 2006 Liz Pichon
CIP data is available
ISBN 1-58925-053-2
Printed in Singapore
1 3 5 7 9 10 8 6 4 2

Bored Bill

by Liz Pichon

 tiger tales

Bill was bored.

He wasn't just a little bored. He was **REALLY, REALLY** bored.

Bill's owner, Mrs. Pickle, was never
bored. She liked to keep busy ALL day.

Mrs. Pickle loved reading.
But Bill thought reading
was boring.

Mrs. Pickle adored gardening.
Bill thought gardening was as
dull as dirt.

Mrs. Pickle was a fantastic cook and a kung fu expert.
"Try this, Bill. It's fun!" she said.
"No way," Bill grumbled.

Mrs. Pickle also liked to do lots of cleaning.
"I'm so bored I can't even move," said Bill.

How boring
is this?

"Come on, Bill. Let's go for a lovely long walk," Mrs. Pickle said.

"Borrrrrring," muttered Bill.

"Only boring dogs get bored," said Mrs. Pickle. "Besides, it's no fun sitting around all day doing nothing."

"I won't go," said Bill firmly.

Outside the weather was horrible.
It was cold and windy. It was so windy
that Mrs. Pickle's hat flew off.
"Whoops!" Mrs. Pickle said, laughing.
"How borrring," groaned Bill.

Suddenly, a huge gust of wind swept down and lifted them both off their feet.

"Yippeeee!" squealed Mrs. Pickle as she disappeared from sight. Bill clung to a tree when—

SNAP! —the branch broke and he was spun up into the air.

Higher and higher he went. Faster and faster, he shot past the moon and stars and way up into space.

"At last!" cheered Bill. "No more boring walks for me. Space will be REALLY exciting."

THUMP!

Bill landed on a strange purple planet.

The noise woke the aliens, who all popped up to see what it was. Bill was thrilled to meet them.

"This planet looks like fun," he said. "I bet Mrs. Pickle isn't having an adventure like this!"

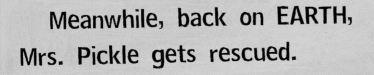

Meanwhile, back on EARTH, Mrs. Pickle gets rescued.

Bill asked the aliens to show him the whole planet.
"LET'S EXPLORE AND HAVE FUN!" Bill shouted.
"What's the point of exploring?" the aliens asked.
"Exploring is boring."
"I'm hungry," one alien mumbled. So they all went
to get something to eat.

"Fantastic!" said Bill. "Alien food MUST be delicious."

But it wasn't. Their slimy green food was **DISGUSTING!** Worse still, the aliens ate it for every single meal.

Life with the aliens was not interesting at all. They just sat around all day long doing absolutely **NOTHING.**

Bill had never been so bored.
He really missed Mrs. Pickle
and her delicious food.

So bored...

Bill looked at the aliens lying around the planet.
Mrs. Pickle was right, he thought suddenly.
Doing nothing all day is REALLY BORING! We need
to get BUSY.

"Come on!" Bill shouted to the aliens. "Only boring aliens get bored. It's time to have some fun!"

Bill cooked the aliens a yummy meal just like Mrs. Pickle's.

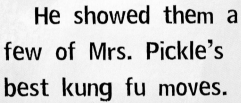

He showed them a few of Mrs. Pickle's best kung fu moves.

Then they played some games, which everyone enjoyed.

NOBODY was bored anymore.
But Bill still missed Mrs. Pickle.
He wanted to go home.

So the aliens brought out their spaceship and flew Bill back down to Earth. They all waved and said goodbye.

When Bill landed, he discovered he was FAMOUS!

EVERYONE wanted to talk to Bill about the aliens. But the only person Bill wanted to see was...

Mrs. Pickle!

"I'll never be bored again!" said Bill as he hugged Mrs. Pickle.

From that day on, Bill always kept himself busy, just like Mrs. Pickle did. He read books and practiced kung fu.

He dug in the garden and cooked delicious food.

Bill even enjoyed doing the cleaning, which Mrs. Pickle thought was very helpful...

especially when
they had so many
new friends visiting!

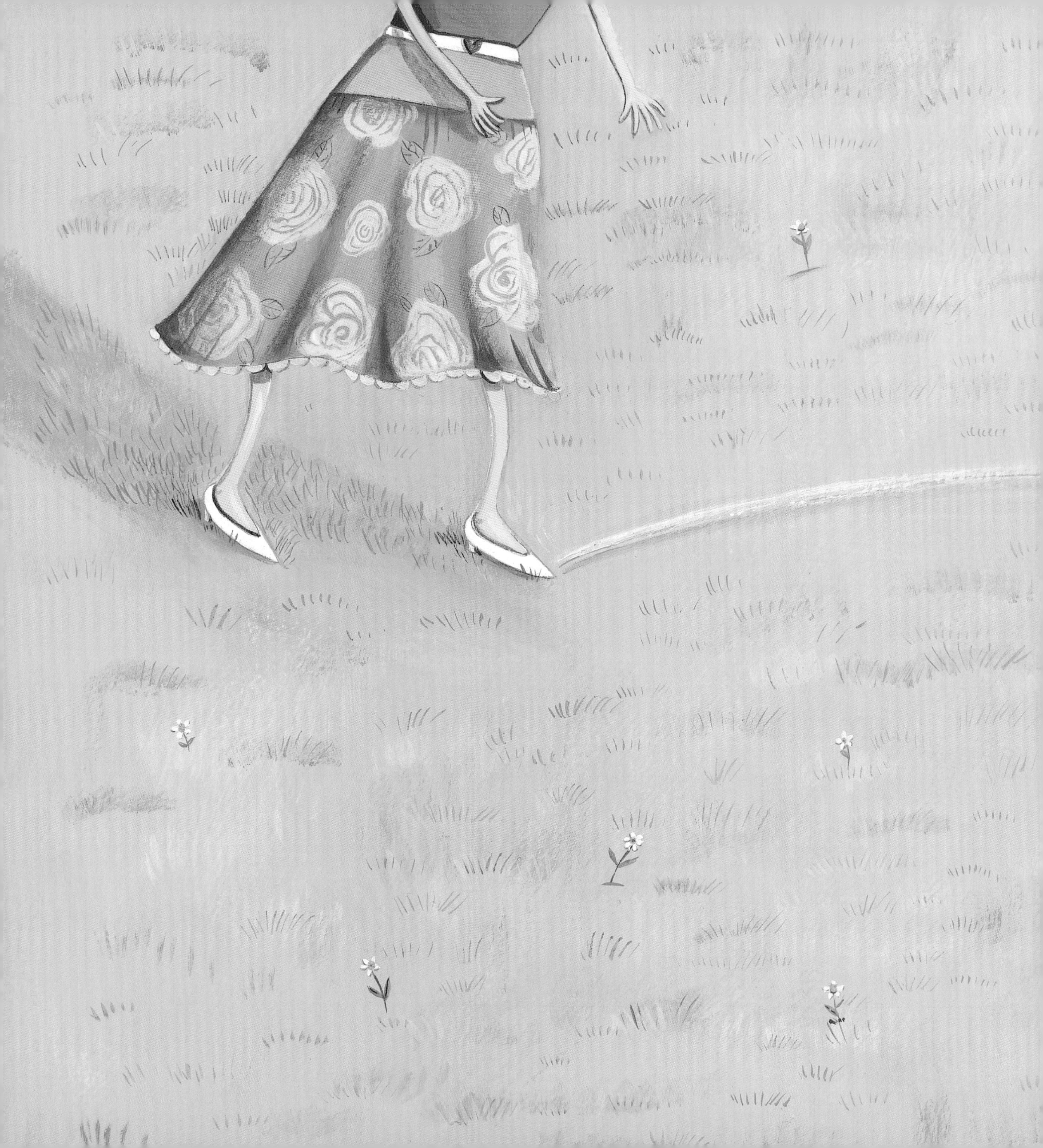